David and the Worry Beast

Helping Children Cope with Anxiety

Anne Marie Guanci

Illustrations by Caroline Attia

New Horizon Press
Far Hills, New Jersey

Dedication

For Jackie, Valerie and David, the loves of my life. And for
Sister Marie, my angel.

New Horizon Press
P.O. Box 669
Far Hills, NJ 07931

Guanci, Anne Marie
Illustrations by Attia, Caroline
David and the Worry Beast:: *Helping Children Cope with Anxiety*

Cover Design: Norma Rahn
Interior Design: Chris Nielsen

Library of Congress Control Number:

ISBN 13: 978-0-88282-275-4
ISBN 10: 0-88282-275-6

SMALL HORIZONS
A Division of New Horizon Press

2011   2010   2009   2008   2007   /   5   4   3   2   1

Printed in Hong Kong

Twenty seconds left in the basketball game...
David had the ball. He wanted to pass it so badly. He looked to the
left, and then to the right. No one was clear...

"It's all up to me," he murmered. "I have to try." He threw the basketball at the hoop as hard as he could. "Oh please go in, please, please," he said softly.

He could feel his heart pounding. The next few seconds felt like hours. As the buzzer sounded, the ball bounced off the rim, missing the net entirely. David's team lost the game.

His teammates groaned loudly. The other team cheered wildly. David felt terrible. Some of the kids shook their heads disgustedly at him. Some just didn't look at him at all.

His friend John said, "Tough luck, David."

In the locker room, after the game, Coach Smith said, "You all played very well. I am proud of all of you. The next game will be for the championship. I know we can win." On the way out, the coach patted David on the back. He smiled at him and said, "Good try, Dave."

David looked down at his feet and sighed, "We lost because of me."

"David," the coach replied, "It's not if you win or lose. The important thing is how you play the game."

"You are just being nice," David said.

As David changed clothes he felt worse and worse. Putting his sneakers in his gym bag, he spied a small furry creature resting on top of his towel.

"What is that?" David said to himself. "It must be one of my sister's stuffed animals." The creature widened his eyes and shook its head. Feeling afraid, David quickly zipped his gym bag closed and left.

David wanted to go home as fast as he could.

At dinner, David's mom and dad each gave him a hug.

"You played a great game. Don't worry about missing that basket," his mom said.

David couldn't stop worrying. He had disappointed his whole team.

"I really messed up. The whole team was counting on me," he said. "I let them down. I don't want to play anymore..."

David's parents tried to comfort him. Their kind words didn't make David feel any better, though.

Later, in his room, David lay in bed, unable to sleep. Suddenly, his gym bag fell off his desk. David jumped up and ran over to it. As he picked it up, he noticed the seams were bulging! Bits of fur popped through the zipper!

David opened the bag.

Out came the furry creature, at least twenty times larger than before.

"I'm your Worry Beast. I'm here so you will worry more and more," the creature said in a scary voice.

"You can't stay here," said David. "You'll have to get in the closet."

The Worry Beast slinked away to the closet. When David finally fell asleep, he had horrible dreams. He kept seeing the Worry Beast growing larger and larger.

David's alarm clock rang early the next morning. He pulled on his clothes and went to breakfast. His mom had brought him his favorite cereal, Frosty Crunch, and even made him hot cocoa. David wasn't hungry.

David sat quietly and stared out the window as his mom drove him to school. He just wanted to forget about the stupid basketball game. Finally he said, "Do I have to play basketball? I don't really want to be on the team anymore, Mom."

"You have always loved basketball, David. Why don't we talk about it later?" answered his mom.

David slowly walked into school feeling miserable. He liked his teacher, Miss Kelly, but he hadn't slept well, so he felt tired.

Johnny, his best friend, sat down next to him. Maybe he'd ask Johnny to come over his house to play. *We can play outside and leave the stupid Worry Beast in the closet*, thought David.

Suddenly, Miss Kelly announced, "There will be a math test tomorrow. You all need to study hard."

"Math test?" muttered David. "I'm not good at math."

David forgot all about asking Johnny over to play. Now he was even more worried than before.

He went back to class where Miss Kelly began to talk about multiplication and division. It was hard, really hard to understand. David was afraid to ask questions when he didn't understand something. The other kids will think I'm dumb, he thought.

"What if I fail the math test? What if my team loses again because of me?" he softly cried.

David was so worried, his stomach ached. He felt like crying.

David raised his hand. "I feel sick. I want to go home," he said.

"Then David, you will need to go to the nurse's office," Miss Kelly said.

"What seems to be the problem, David?" asked Nurse Mary when she saw him.

David clutched at his stomach. "I feel like I want to throw up. I want to go home," said David.

"Upset belly, huh?" asked Nurse Mary. She popped a thermometer in his mouth. When it beeped, Nurse Mary took it out, looked at the reading, and said, "Hmm...No fever, but something is wrong for sure. Is something worrying you, David? Sometimes kids feel ill if they have big worries on their minds."

David still was silent. He didn't want to look at Nurse Mary for fear she would see he was terribly worried. He didn't want to talk about it. He only wanted the worry to go away.

"It's true," Nurse Mary continued, "I have seen worries grow so big that they take right over. Are you worried about something, David?"

David shook his head and asked, "May I go home now?"

"Wait here, I'll call your mom," Nurse Mary replied.

Nurse Mary called David's mom and asked her to come to the school to pick up David. She also asked David's mom to check in with Miss Vivian, the school psychologist, before taking David home.

"I think David's stomach is upset, because he is keeping worries bottled up inside," Nurse Mary explained.

When she arrived at the school, David's mom walked over to Miss Vivian's office.

"Sometimes children feel so worried that they feel sick. Sometimes children get upset stomachs. Some get headaches. Some get both! Others feel nervous and fearful a lot of the time," said Miss Vivian. "They almost never want to talk about their worries at first."

"Last night David told me how badly he felt about missing the basket during the game. Are you also worried about something else, David?" his mom asked.

David looked down at the floor and didn't say a word.

Miss Vivian looked at David and asked, "Do you want to talk about how you are feeling?"

David shook his head.

"What can we do to help David when he feels worried?" asked his mom.

"David needs to know that he can talk about the things troubling him. Check with him often." She looked over at the boy, "David, remember that you can always talk to your parents when something bothers you," said Miss Vivian.

"Here is a CD that might make you feel better when you are upset. You can listen to it at bedtime or anytime you feel worried. It has soothing music and peaceful sounds which will help you relax. There are some ocean sounds. Do you like the beach, David?" asked Miss Vivian.

"I love the beach and especially swimming," David replied, smiling for the first time.

"Good," answered Miss Vivian. "Then you will enjoy this CD. Come back and see me soon."

Walking to the car, David felt a little better, but he was quiet again as his mom drove home.

"In the next game you'll score," his mom said, smiling at him when she stopped for a red light.

David's stomach started to churn again.

As soon as they got home, David wanted to go to his room and lie in bed with a pillow over his head. He wanted to forget about the math test, forget about the basketball tournament and forget about going to school...just forget about everything!

When his mom pulled the car into the driveway, David saw a terrible sight and shrieked.

The Worry Beast David had tucked into his closet had grown so big! Its furry head popped through the roof. One furry arm stuck out of David's bedroom window.

"What am I going to do?" David asked.

He looked around and saw a crowd gathering on the lawn of the house.

Someone must have called for help. A police car and a fire truck arrived at the scene. The policeman and fireman ran over, pushed through the crowd and looked in amazement at the furry creature bulging out of David's house. They scratched their heads in disbelief. "I've never seen anything like this before," David heard the policeman say. "Neither have I," said the fireman.

"The Worry Beast is huge and I do not know what to do! How can I make my worries stop growing and go away?" David asked.

Just then David's dad came home from work. Scrambling out of his car, he ran toward his family. "What is that?" he asked   frantically, pointing at the giant creature.

"It's my Worry Beast. He just keeps getting bigger and bigger, and it won't go away!" David answerwed.

Putting his arm around his son, "Why are you so worried, son? Talk to us."

David remembered what Miss Vivian and Nurse Mary had said about sharing your feelings with a grown-up.

"I missed the shot!" said David. "I missed the shot and lost the game for the team. Now I'm worried that I'll do it again. I'm not even sure I want to play basketball anymore."

"It's okay to be a little nervous, David," his dad said. "Remember, a team wins together and a team loses together. No one person causes a team to win or lose."

"The important part is having fun while doing your best," added his mom.

"It's not about being the best or winning every game," said David's dad. "It's about trying hard and being a good sport."

David thought about his dad's words.

"You are right," said David.

He ran up to his room and shouted to the Worry Beast, "I'll play in the basketball tournament! I'll have fun! If my team doesn't win, it's okay!"

Through the windows, the crowd watched in amazement as the Worry Beast began to shrink. They all clapped their hands and some shouted, "Good job."

Back outside with his parents, David remembered he was also worried about the math test.

"Are you worried about something else?" David's mom asked him.

"I have a math test tomorrow," said David. "I don't understand how to multiply and divide very well. I am afraid that if I ask for help, the other kids will think that I am dumb."

"It is never dumb to ask for help," said his dad. "That is how you learn new things. Just do your best."

David walked up the stairs and into his room. He saw the Beast standing in a corner. He ran over and bravely looked the Worry Beast in the eye.

"I have a math test tomorrow. I'll study hard and do my best. My best is good enough!" said David.

Suddenly, the Worry Beast began shrinking until he disappeared. David's room was no longer stuffed with worry.

"I beat the Worry Beast!" David called to his mom and dad.

David's parents ran upstairs and sat down next to him.

"David, this is the best news yet. We are so proud of you," said his mom.

The next day, David and his parents met with Miss Vivian again at school. David told her how his worry grew and grew until the Worry Beast came to live in his closet.

With Miss Vivian's help, David finally learned how to stop his thoughts from making a little worry into a giant Worry Beast. One way David learned to stop bad thoughts was by picturing a big red stop sign. Then he would say to himself, "Even if this is a big worry I can handle it. If I can't stop my worry, I can get mom, dad and my teachers to help me."

Miss Vivian also taught him a breathing exercise to relax, "Take a deep breath through your nose whenever you feel anxious and slowly let it out through your mouth."

David tried the exercise. He did it very well.

Miss Vivian nodded and smiled at him.

Miss Vivian said, "Don't avoid your worries. Always talk to someone you trust like a parent or teacher."

David told her, "I am not going to quit the team."

Miss Vivian patted David on the back. "That is a very good decision," she said.

During their final game his team didn't win the championship, but David played well. David felt proud of himself. He had stuck with the team even though he felt scared. His parents said he was very brave.

Coach Smith said, "Our team played like champions even though we lost. Next year we will try again and I believe we will win."

For the first time David felt good even though his team had lost.

But David had a new worry that night. He had a project due the next morning on Native Americans. He started to worry that maybe he should do the drawings of the teepees over again to make them look better. Just then David saw the furry Worry Beast pop out of his closet.

"Not you again," David said.

David hit the play button on his CD player and heard the calming sounds Miss Vivian had described. He closed his eyes and did the breathing exercise she taught him. He took a deep breath in through his nose and then slowly let it out through his mouth. David did this three times, then calmly faced the Worry Beast.

"My project is fine, I tried my best. If it isn't perfect, it is okay!" said David.

Suddenly, the Worry Beast vanished into thin air.

THE END

Tips for Kids:

1. You are not alone. Lots of kids worry about school, sports and other activities, as well as friends and family problems.

2. You can learn ways to help yourself feel better when you are upset.

3. If you don't understand something, don't be embarrassed to ask your parent or teacher questions about the problem and tell them how you are feeling.

4. It is okay to feel unsure of yourself when doing something new or scary.

5. Share your scared feelings with a parent or trusted grown-up. Talking with a teacher or school counselor can help you feel better.

6. Remember, no one is perfect. You don't need to be the best at everything.

7. Feel proud of yourself each time you try your hardest.

8. To keep your worries from growing too large, picture a big, red stop sign in front of you. Stop at the sign and think for a few minutes about your problem. Is it large, medium or small?

9. Try this deep breathing exercise when you are very worried about a problem: Take a deep breath in through your nose. Then slowly let it out through your mouth. Do this a few times; it will help your body relax.

10. Listen to soothing music or peaceful sounds at bedtime or before a big game or test. This will help you relax and take your mind off feeling anxious or worried.

Tips for Parents:

1. Have realistic expectations of your child's academic and extracurricular achievements.

2. Acknowledge and praise your child's efforts rather than the outcome.

3. Remember the main thing is that your child tries his/her best.

4. Acknowledge his/her fear. Help your child keep anxiety in perspective through reality questioning. Is this mountain really a molehill?

5. Verbalize your confidence in your child and offer support.

6. Resist the temptation to support avoidant behavior. Avoiding the cause of anxiety will only heighten the anxiety of the child.

7. Encourage participation and praise the child for being brave.

8. Know the philosophy of your child's coach or team leader. A good coach of young children will emphasize sportsmanship over victory.

9. Make sure your child's anxiety is not the direct result of an adult placing too much pressure on him/her to excel.

10. Encourage your child to do deep breathing exercises or listen to a relaxation CD during times of stress. Practice with him/her.

11. Seek professional counseling should your child's anxiety result in headaches and other physical manifestations of stress including stomachaches, irritable bowel syndrome, low self-esteem, social isolation, inadequate social skills and problems in social adjustment and/or academic work.

I DON'T WANT TO GO TO SCHOOL

Helping Children Cope with Seperation Anxiety

by Nancy J. Pando, L.I.C.S.W.

illustrated by Kathy Voerg

Honey Maloo, a young bee, is finally old enough to attend school. Honey, however, would much rather stay home with her mother, whom she loves dearly. She tries every trick in the book to stay off the school bus. With patience and guidance from her mother and teacher, Honey finally goes to class. As she meets new friends and becomes interested in singing, reading and other activities, Honey finds out that school can be fun and her mom will be waiting for her when she gets home.

Separation anxiety is a common dilemma in children and can make even the briefest of partings excruciating for parents and children alike. Charming, accessible and informative, *I Don't Want to Go to School* offers parents and teachers ways to teach children to cope with separation from loved ones.

Nancy J. Pando, L.I.C.S.W., has a private psychotherapy practice specializing in the treatment of children and adolescents. A guardian ad litem *in the Norfolk and Plymouth County, Massachusetts court systems, she is also the author of* Foster Bug *(FosterClub, 2001). She lives in Canton, Massachusetts.*

Kathy Voerg, a graduate of Pratt Institute, is a freelance illustrator. She resides just outside of New York City in Rutherford, New Jersey.

A New Horizon Press 2005 release
7 x 8 , 48 pages
26 color illustrations
LC# 2004118085
ISBN 13: 978-0-88282-254-9
ISBN: 0-88282-254-3
$8.95

JESSICA'S TWO FAMILIES

Helping Children Cope with Blended Households

by Lynne Hugo

illustrated by Adam Gordon

Like many children from divorced families, Jessica finds herself dealing with the pressures and anger that come when both her parents remarry and she has two whole new families to live with. Her new step-parents set down rules that feel unfair and her new step-siblings don't seem to want her around. Jessica feels lonely because her mother spends time with her new husband and her father is busy with two additional children to raise. With the support of a counselor, Jessica courageously tells her family how she feels. With honesty and compassion, this book teaches children that it is okay to be upset about adjusting to new families. It urges them to share their feelings. Children learn that functioning as blended family will take time, but their efforts will be rewarded.

Lynne Hugo holds a master's degree from Miami University in southwestern Ohio. A Licensed Professional Clinical Counselor, she has worked as a psychotherapist for twenty-five years. The co-author of Swimming Lessons *(William Morrow and Co.) and* Baby's Breath *(Synergistic Press), she resides in Oxford, Ohio with her husband and two children.*

Adam Gordon has been an educational illustrator since graduating from The Rhode Island School of Design in 1986. He lives on Staten Island, NY where he teaches an art class for children.

A New Horizon Press 2005 release
7 x 8 , 48 pages
26 color illustrations
LC# 2004118084
ISBN 13:978-0-88282-263-1
ISBN: 0-88282-263-2
$8.95